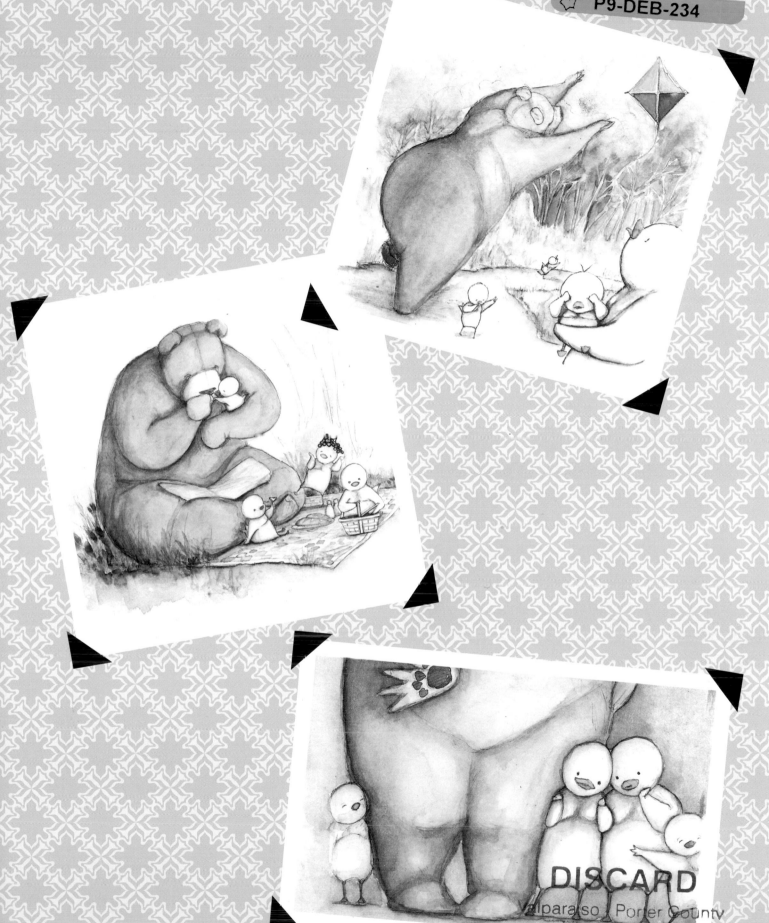

BEAR IS NOT TIRED

Ciara Gavin

Alfred A. Knopf 🐎 New York

For Mam and Dad

THIS IS A BORZOI BOOK PUBLISHED BY ALFRED A. KNOPF

Copyright © 2016 by Ciara Gavin

All rights reserved. Published in the United States by Alfred A. Knopf, an imprint of Random House Children's Books, a division of Penguin Random House LLC, New York.
Knopf, Borzoi Books, and the colophon are registered trademarks of Penguin Random House LLC.

Visit us on the Web! randomhousekids.com
Educators and librarians, for a variety of teaching tools, visit us at RHTeachersLibrarians.com

Library of Congress Cataloging-in-Publication Data
Gavin, Ciara, author, illustrator.
Bear is not tired / Ciara Gavin. — First edition.
pages cm.
Summary: "Bear is supposed to sleep through the winter, but he doesn't want to miss out on any of the fun. Fortunately, Mama Duck comes up with a plan that will help everyone have the perfect winter." —Provided by publisher
ISBN 978-0-385-75476-7 (trade) — ISBN 978-0-385-75477-4 (lib. bdg.) — ISBN 978-0-385-75478-1 (ebook)
[1. Bears—Fiction. 2. Ducks—Fiction. 3. Hibernation—Fiction. 4. Friendship—Fiction. 5. Winter—Fiction.] I. Title.
PZ7.G2354Be 2016
[E]—dc23
2015012009

MANUFACTURED IN MALAYSIA
January 2016
10 9 8 7 6 5 4 3 2 1   First Edition

Bear and the ducks lived together under the
same roof. They were one big happy family.

Sometimes Bear forgot that he wasn't a duck.

He hardly noticed the difference.

Then one morning, there was a sharp chill in the air.
The ducks didn't mind, but the cold tickled Bear's nose.
It could only mean one thing: Winter was coming.

And that meant it was nearly time for Bear to go to sleep.

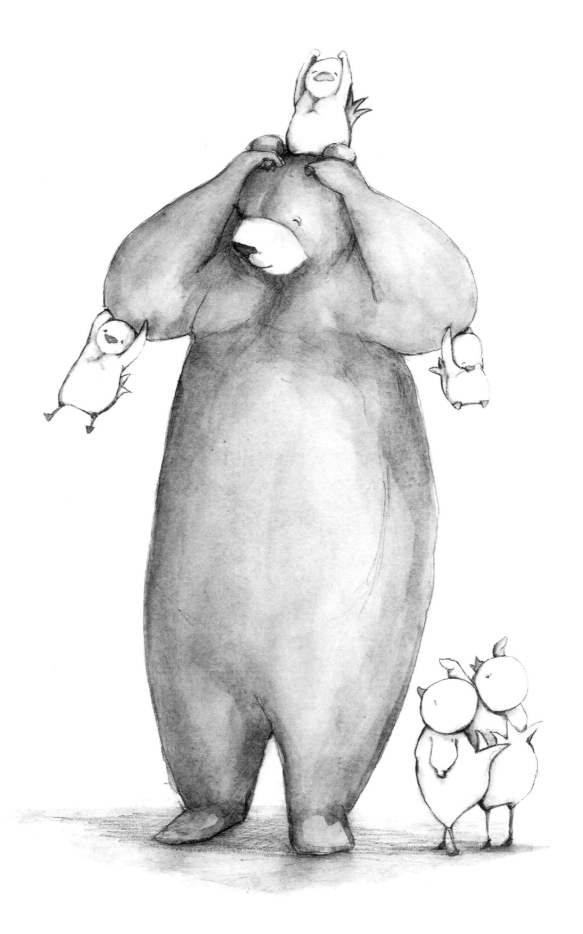

He had been having so much fun, he'd forgotten all about it.

So, Bear decided to stay awake.

After all, he wasn't feeling the *least* bit sleepy.

But the ducks began to notice a change in Bear.

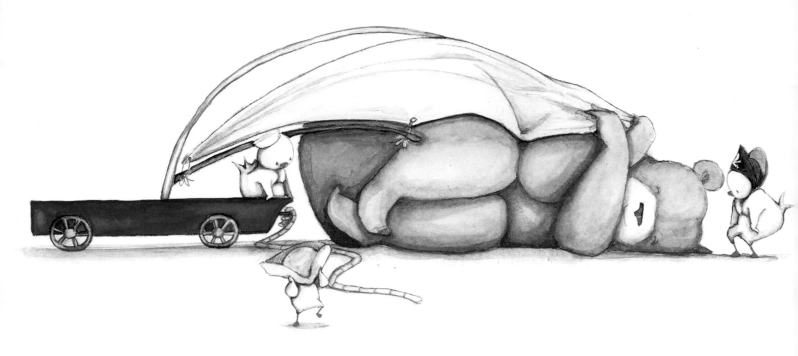

He kept falling asleep at the most inconvenient times.

Bear tried to think of ways to stay awake.

The ducks tried to help him.

But nothing worked.

Every sound was a lullaby.
The rippling of
the water . . .

The hum of
the washing
machine . . .

The *tap, tap, tap* of
Baby Duck's feet.

Bear was so tired, nothing made sense anymore.

Mama Duck said Bear couldn't fight who he was.
Bears are bears, and bears are supposed to sleep in
winter. She promised him he wouldn't miss a thing.

Feeling reassured, Bear finally fell into a deep sleep.

The ducks carried on with
their usual winter activities.

They included Bear whenever they could.

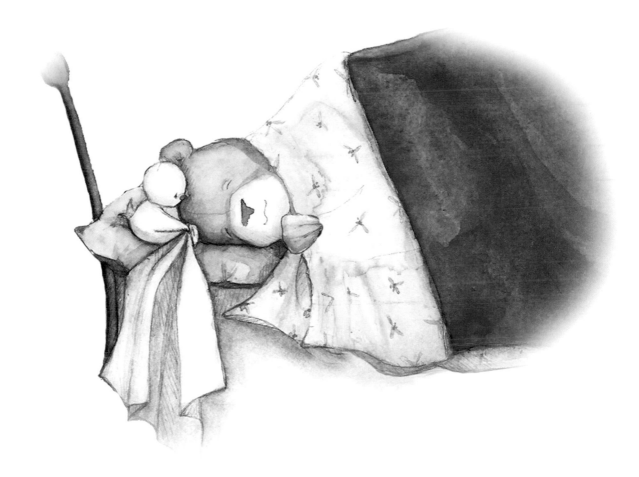

Even Baby Duck found a way to keep him close.

Then one morning, Bear sat up and opened his eyes. It was spring!

And Mama Duck had kept her promise.

She even had the photos to prove it.

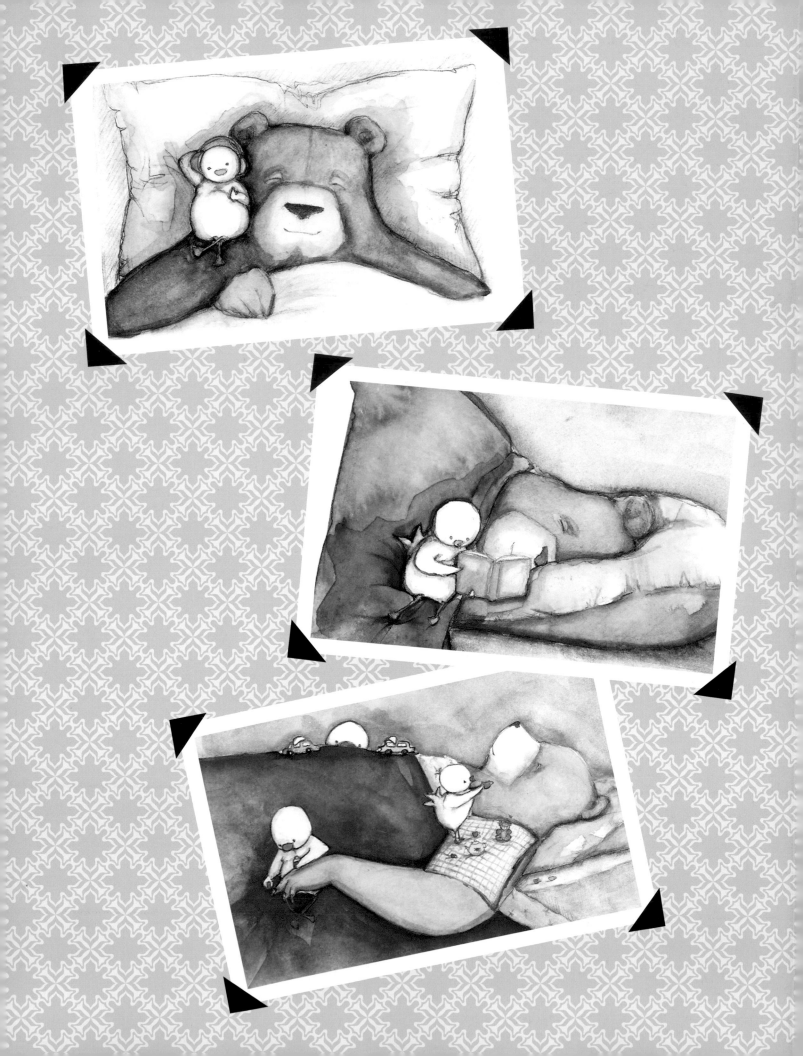